D1511219

For R.J. and C.I.
Mama loves you more.

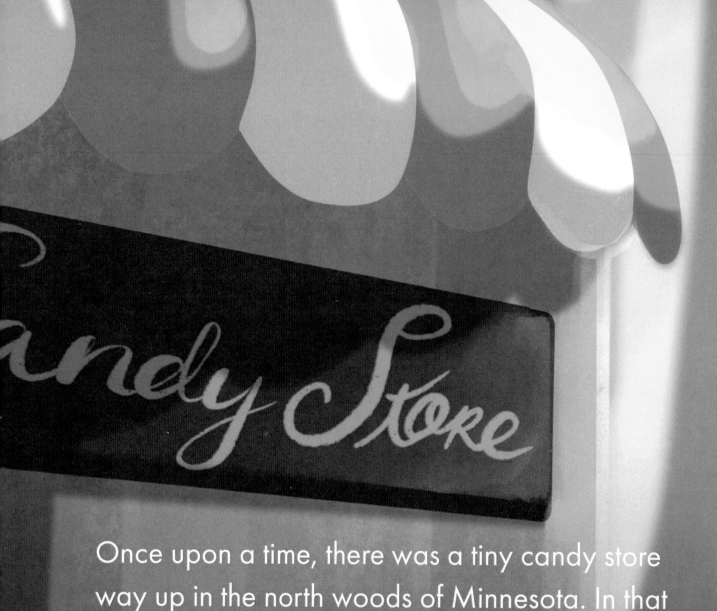

andy Store

Once upon a time, there was a tiny candy store way up in the north woods of Minnesota. In that store lived a little gray wolf, high up on the back of an old shelf.

Every night, when the lady in the store put out the closed sign and went home ...

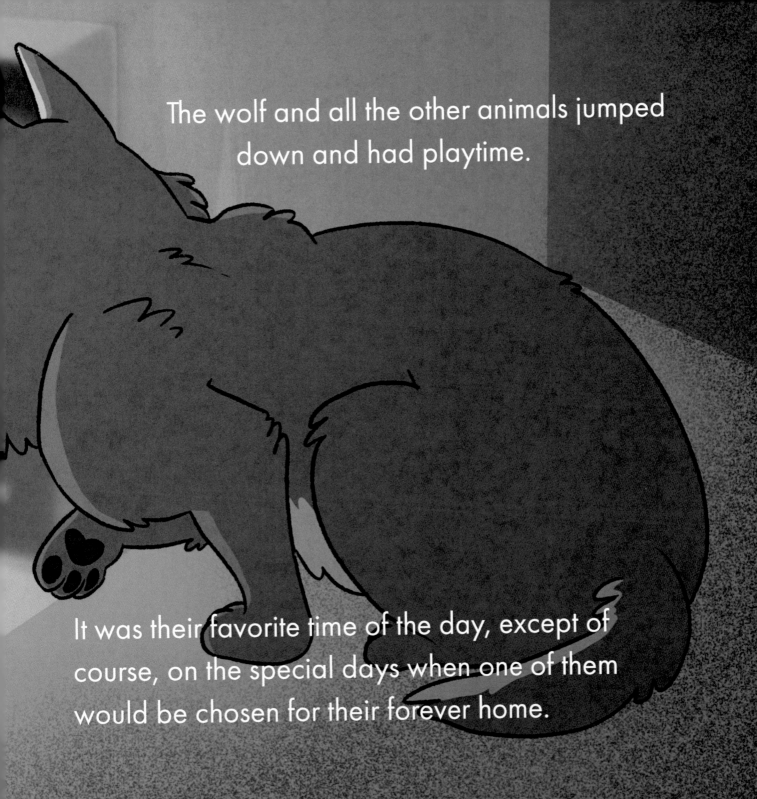

The wolf and all the other animals jumped down and had playtime.

It was their favorite time of the day, except of course, on the special days when one of them would be chosen for their forever home.

A soft, tabby cat named Meow Meow, and Hopper the frog started a game of tag.

Even Tucker the painted turtle and Freddy the guppy fish played! "Little wolf aren't you playing today?" asked Freddy.

No thanks," said the wolf.
The wolf pup was very sad, for he had lived on that dusty old shelf, squeezed behind all the other toys for a long, long time.

Many other animals came and went while he was never picked. Even Digger the lobster found his forever home!

He was so lonely! He wanted his own little person to play with and love. He could just imagine the fun they would have together!

So he waited.
And waited and waited.

Meow Meow the cat liked to tease the little wolf. "Gray Wolf," she said, "you have been here forever and ever!"

"Yeah," Harry the Hedgie chimed in, "no one can even see you behind the rest of us!"

"Aw come on you guys," said Pooch, the fluffy yellow dog, "leave poor little Gray Wolf alone."

Therefore, they did. "I was just kidding him," replied Harry, "sorry dude!"

"It's ok," said the wolf, "I know you didn't mean it!"

Just when he thought the store would be his forever home, an amazing thing happened.

One sunny spring day, after it had just stopped raining, the front door of the shop jingled.

A little girl with bright yellow pigtails bounced in right behind her mama and dad. She was smiling from ear to ear.

"This is the best trip ever!" she exclaimed to her parents. **"I love it here!"**

"Oh man," the little gray wolf thought,
"her family just stopped in for treats."

So he curled up in a ball where he had
been napping and went back to sleep.
He slept and slept, dreaming about playing
outside in the woods.

"Mama, I want that one,"
he woke to hear. "Not that
one...**THAT one!**"

"Scoopies, are you sure my love? Look at
this crazy, cute froggy," said the mama,
"you love frogs!"

"Positively positive," said the girl,
"he needs a home with us!"

Suddenly, the little gray wolf felt himself moving. Wait. What was happening? Was he still dreaming? He was slowly being lifted down the shelf from way up high and placed in the girl's arms.

She smelled like sunshine and chocolate chip cookies. **It was the best feeling ever!**

"Ohhhh what a cute little woofy!" the little girl exclaimed. The wolf pup could not believe his ears. Was she talking about him?

"Please, please can we take him home?" she begged. "Ryley, you have so many other stuffed toys at home," her dad replied. "How about some Hot Air candy?"

"Daddy, if I can have this I will never, ever, ever ask for any treats EVER again. I promise!"

The gray wolf's heart started to leap. He saw the mama talk to the dad. The dad chuckled and turned toward the little blonde girl, who was still holding him tight.

"Well," he said, "then I guess we better take him home." "Oh, thank you!" said Ryley. The little gray wolf felt like crying.

He was so happy!

Then the girl with the bouncy blonde pigtails and a big smile on her face did something amazing. "I am going to name him Woofy," she said. "We will have lots of adventures, and I will love him forever."

"Wolfy?" the mama asked.
"Yep!" said Ryley as she gave him a smooch.
"He will always be my Woofy Toofy!"

And the little girl with blonde pigtails and the stuffed gray wolf became fast friends.

She tucked him under her armpit. Together, Ryley and Woofy walked out of the store in the woods and on to their next adventure.

For there would be many adventures to come.